This dragon book belongs to:

....

D1194507

Teach Your Dragon Good Hygiene
My Dragon Books - Volume 32
Written by Steve Herman

Copyright © 2019 by Digital Golden Solutions LLC.
Published by DG Books Publishing, an imprint of Digital Golden Solutions LLC.

All rights reserved. No part of this publication may be reproduced, distributed, or transmitted in any form or by any means, including photocopying, recording, or other electronic or mechanical methods, without the prior written permission of the publisher, except in the case of brief quotations embodied in critical reviews and certain other noncommercial uses permitted by copyright law.

Information contained within this book is for entertainment and educational purposes only. Although the author and publisher have made every effort to ensure that the information in this book was correct at press time, the author and publisher do not assume and hereby disclaim any liability to any party for any loss, damage, or disruption caused by errors or omissions, whether such errors or omissions result from negligence, accident, or any other cause.

ISBN: 978-1950280148 (paperback)
ISBN: 978-1950280155 (hardcover)

www.MyDragonBooks.com

First Edition: September 2019
10 9 8 7 6 5 4 3 2 1

Teach Your Dragon Good Hygiene

My Dragon Books - Volume 32

Steve Herman

Well, hello there! It's us again,
Drew and Diggory Doo –
A kid and his pet dragon
with another book for you.

We started writing books back
when Diggory Doo was small,
All about his growing up –
We hope you've liked them all.

From the bad breath in his dragon snout down to his stinky feet, It takes a lot of scrubbing to keep Diggory smelling sweet.

Then he began to notice
that wherever he would go,
Folks would walk the other way,
but Diggory didn't know

"Soap gets in my eyes!" he said.
"The water is too hot!
When I get out, I catch a chill.
Please, Drew, I'd rather not!"

"Every time you take a bath,
please put on fresh, clean clothes,"

"Then, instead of smelling bad, you'll be smelling like a rose."

"And several times a day,
give your hands a soapy scrub,
Then you can be a member
of the clean and healthy club!"

"How can germs be bad?" he asked.
"They're small and can't be seen!
I like to play and hate to stop.
Why must I be so clean?"

When we discussed his dental health,
he had a new excuse –
Diggory asked, "Why should I brush?
I just don't see the use..."

AT LEAST TWO TIMES A DAY!

I added, "You should brush your teeth
at least two times a day
To keep them clean and healthy,
and then folks won't run away

"Being clean is healthy.
Now, Diggory can you see
How important HYGIENE is
and keeping clean can be?"

"Though Diggory made excuses, it didn't take him very long When he listened to my reasons to see that he'd been wrong."

Now he has good HYGIENE,
for he learned his lesson well –
"Don't go spreading germs around;
keep clean so you don't smell!"

But these are not just habits that a dragon needs to do –
Do you know who else needs HYGIENE?
That's right! **YOU** need it, too!

Read more about Drew and Diggory Doo!

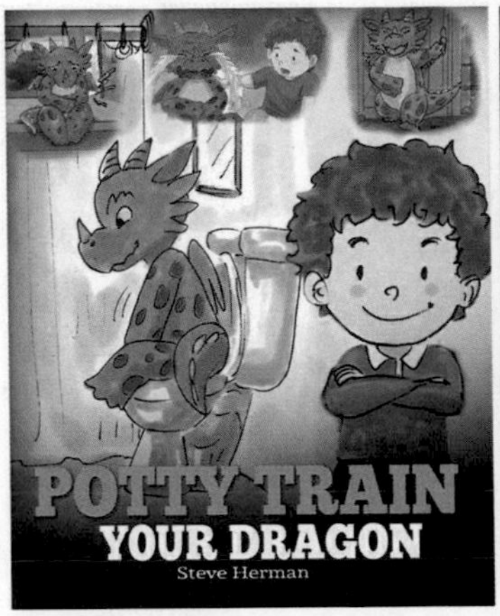
POTTY TRAIN
YOUR DRAGON
Steve Herman

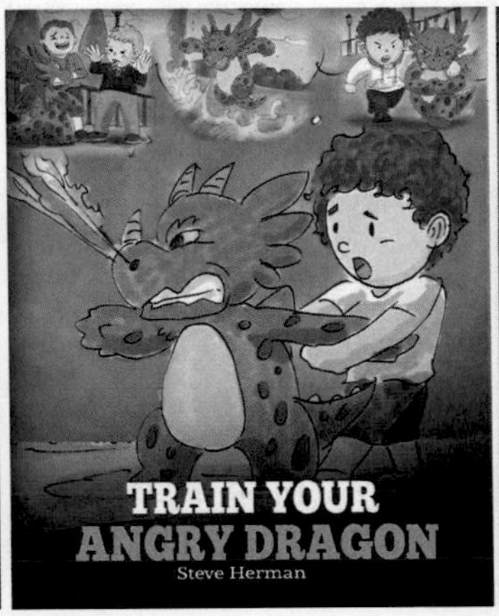
TRAIN YOUR
ANGRY DRAGON
Steve Herman

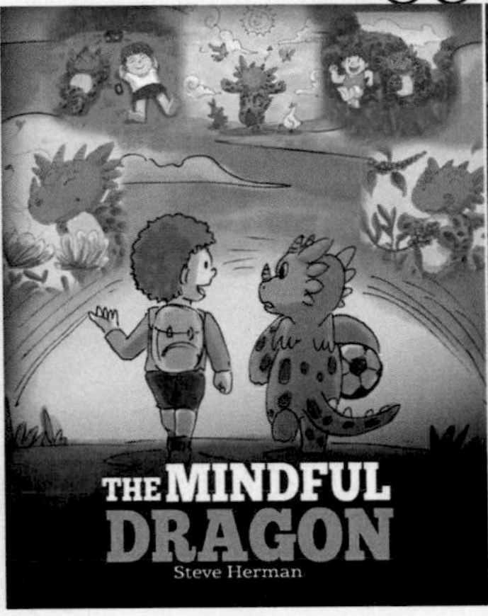
THE MINDFUL
DRAGON
Steve Herman

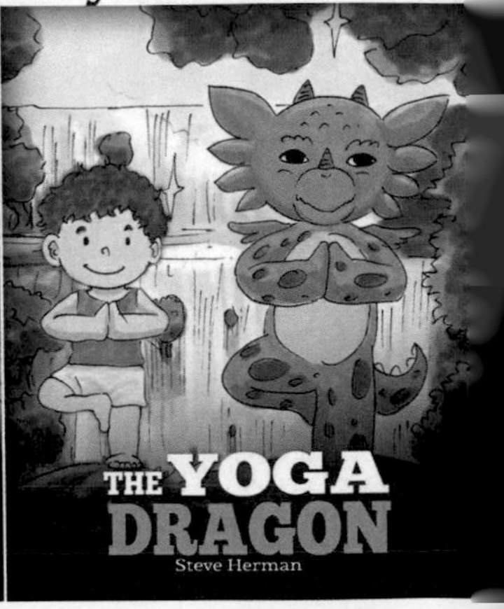
THE YOGA
DRAGON
Steve Herman

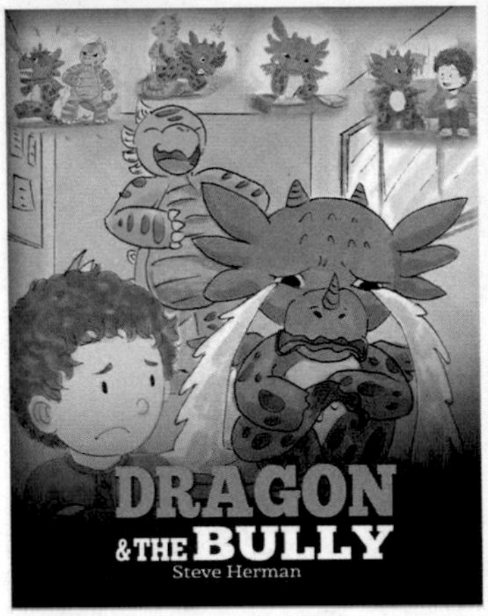
DRAGON
& THE BULLY
Steve Herman

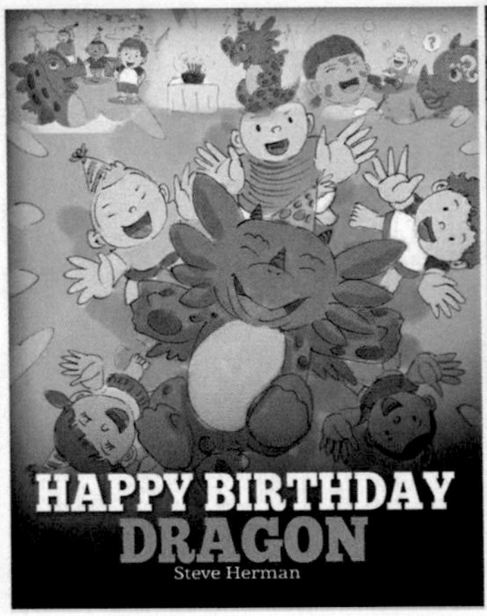
HAPPY BIRTHDAY
DRAGON
Steve Herman

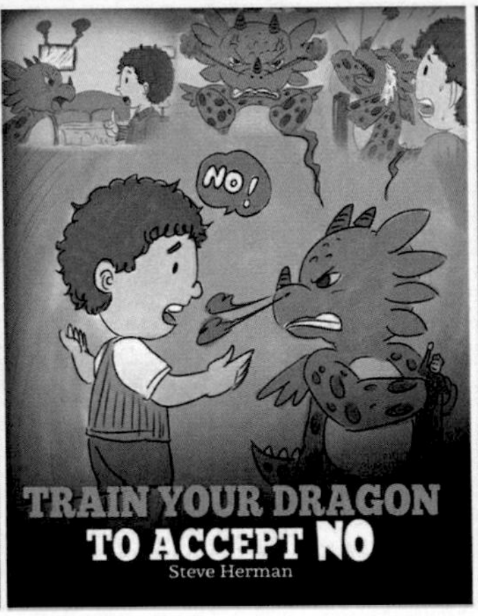
NO!
TRAIN YOUR DRAGON
TO ACCEPT NO
Steve Herman

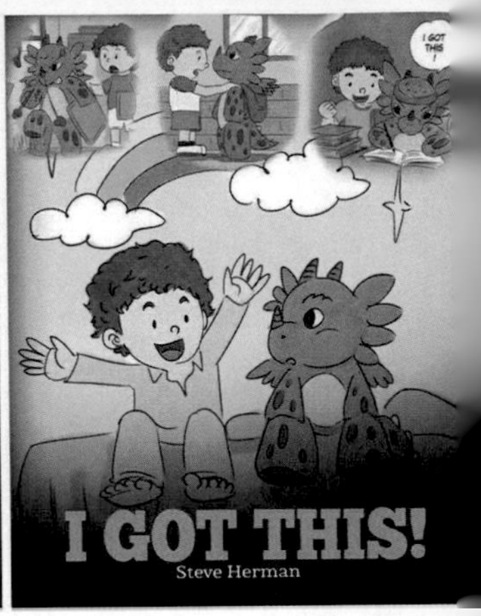
I GOT THIS!
Steve Herman

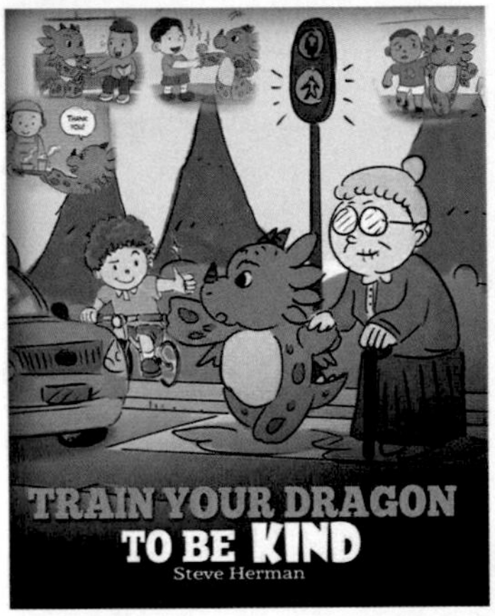
TRAIN YOUR DRAGON
TO BE KIND
Steve Herman

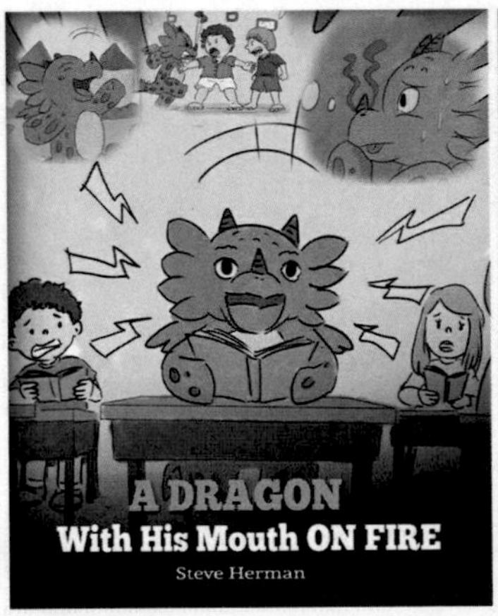
A DRAGON
With His Mouth ON FIRE
Steve Herman

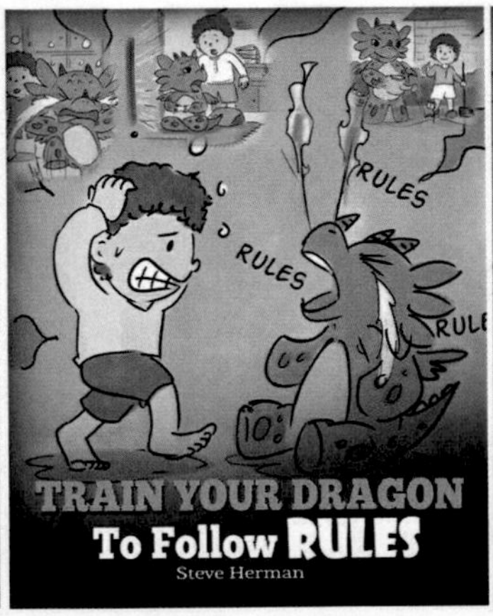
RULES
RULES
TRAIN YOUR DRAGON
To Follow RULES
Steve Herman

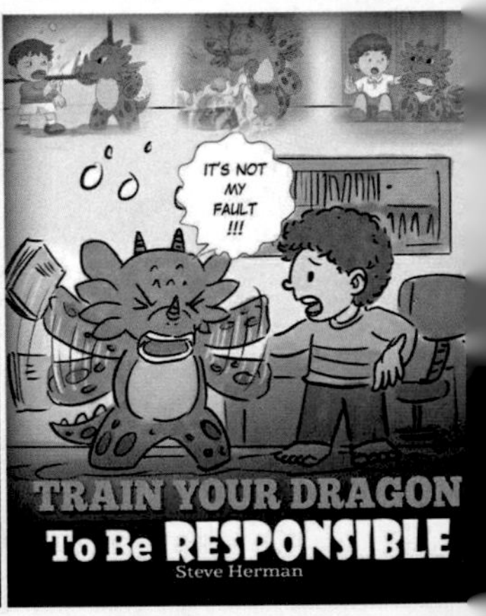
IT'S NOT MY FAULT !!!
TRAIN YOUR DRAGON
To Be RESPONSIBLE
Steve Herman

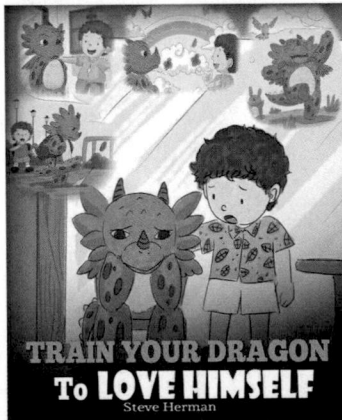

TRAIN YOUR DRAGON
To LOVE HIMSELF
Steve Herman

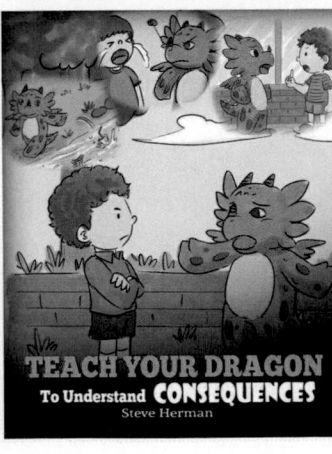

TEACH YOUR DRAGON
To Understand CONSEQUENCES
Steve Herman

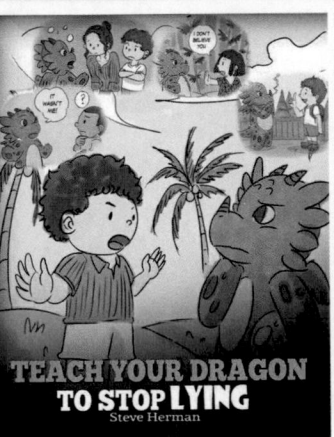

TEACH YOUR DRAGON
TO STOP LYING
Steve Herman

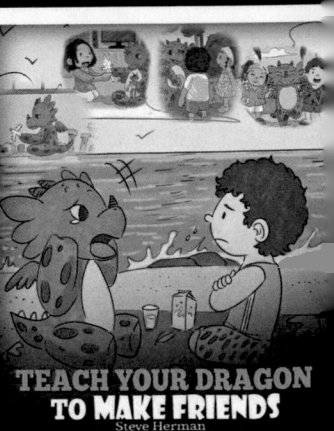

TEACH YOUR DRAGON
TO MAKE FRIENDS
Steve Herman

Visit www.MyDragonBooks.com for more!

TEACH YOUR DRAGON TO SHARE
Steve Herman

FIX YOUR DRAGON'S ATTITUDE
Steve Herman

GET YOUR DRAGON TO TRY NEW THINGS
Steve Herman

TEACH YOUR DRAGON TO FOLLOW INSTRUCTIONS
Steve Herman

HELP YOUR DRAGON DEAL WITH ANXIETY
Steve Herman

A DRAGON CHRISTMAS
Steve Herman

TEACH YOUR DRAGON MANNERS
Steve Herman

TEACH YOUR DRAGON EMPATHY
Steve Herman

TEACH YOUR DRAGON About DIVERSITY
Steve Herman

HELP YOUR DRAGON Learn From MISTAKES
Steve Herman

HELP YOUR DRAGON DEAL WITH CHANGE
Steve Herman

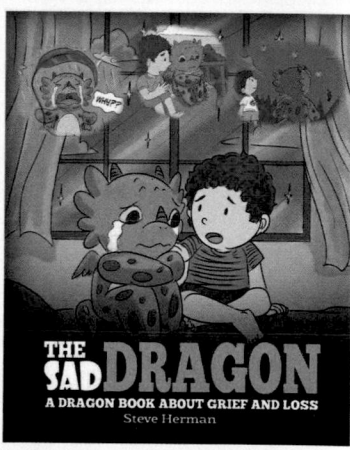

THE SAD DRAGON
A DRAGON BOOK ABOUT GRIEF AND LOSS
Steve Herman

DRAGON SIBLING RIVALRY
Steve Herman

LIMIT YOUR DRAGON'S SCREEN TIME
Steve Herman

DRAGON and HIS FRIEND
A Dragon Book About Autism
Steve Herman

TEACH YOUR DRAGON GOOD HYGIENE
Steve Herman

Get your FREE gift
from Diggory Doo at
www.MyDragonBooks.com/gift